The Surfer's Portal

by

Luis Girado

For Inés

Acknowledgements

In appreciation for the encouragement and support
that my wife, my kids and my friends give me when
I write. You are my source of inspiration.
Thank you.

Contents

A Lifetime Ride

Hobe Sound, Florida, September 4th, 2011.

Today is the day that I will go through the Portal.

I've been waiting for it since November 15th, 1959, when I was 15 years old and my body was slim and flexible, my surf style smooth and flawless. I was never eclectic or clumsy in my runs. Each movement that I made showed harmony and coordination. I could flow with the waves like no one else because I understood our lives are like them. Each wave is an individual, each ride is unique. Every run teaches us something, and when it's over, we go back to the one and same ocean. But now I am 67 years old and my body is stiff and my surf style is clumsy. I have preferred to go easy on my rides to avoid facing my limits. I have become lazy and let the opportunities for a good ride pass me by.

"Oh, there will be others…", I say.

Even more, there is also my right knee pain which makes me limp a little when I walk and stand too high when I surf. My hands are spotted with freckles and get swollen with cold. I have no hair left on my head, except for a ridiculous mini pony tail that I wear, that looks like it is saying "I am still here, inside".

Today is the date that stuck in my memory 52 years ago, but I still do not know why. It takes 25 minutes to walk to the spot. The road only makes it halfway up the island, so I need to walk the rest of the way on the beach. I also know this by memory.
I come on my own with my best surfboard, which I take out of the car in the dusty parking lot, and start the walk at 7:30 am. The day is breaking and the ocean looks pretty calm, nothing extraordinary. Actually, I think, nothing is particular about this day at all, but still, I keep on walking towards my preset time and place with curiosity and tremendous faith. 25 minutes pass by and I have a feeling of familiarity with the place.

"This is it", I say as if reassuring myself. I see a long curvy beach and the pointy sand bar at the end. This is the place, I am certain.

The routine starts. Stretching with effort, I try to reach my toes when I bend. No way I can reach them.

"Bahhh… I just need a little more time to get ready, that's it." I say to myself.

As I turn to twist my waist, I see another surfer coming from my same direction, walking towards me. She is an older woman in a dark, worn out wet suit. She starts the stretching routine in silence, away from me. I notice she takes her time, like she is thinking about it. Her hair is white and her body is skinny. She looks close to my age.

I wrap the strap to my ankle and walk into the ocean with my surfboard in hand. The water feels cold when I throw myself on top of the board and start paddling. Five minutes later, I am behind the breakers, sitting on the board while I watch the lady paddling towards my same spot. I can tell she was an expert surfer by the way she uses little strength to get through the waves. She passes me by without a word and goes further on, way beyond me.

For some reason I follow her, and we both paddle into the deep sea, where the water feels cooler and looks darker. We paddle even further, and when I turn to see the beach I only see a thin yellow line in the horizon, but still, for some reason, I do not stop I just follow her.

Suddenly she sits up and turns her board.

"Come on!", she yells, "here she comes!"

I follow her again, but I do not dare to watch the ocean. I can feel it coming, though. Butterflies flotter in my stomach.

"Quick!" she urges me and paddles sideways. "It will break that way."

I follow.

"Faster, faster!", she screams desperately. I notice how little strength she has left in her elderly body. I am very tired too. My knee hurts badly.

"Come on!" she yells again, with a sigh.

"Come...on.." she tries to encourage me again.

She is giving it all, and I follow.

A deep blue, fresh, pure, and pristine wave is elevating our surfboards. It is preparing us for the ride of our lives, charging us with an energy like I have never felt before. We paddle faster and faster, and our arms are transforming that energy into strength. We are going so fast, that the boards show a white wake tracing through the round top of the wave. Now, our legs, too, move faster and faster, battling the water. I can feel my board already on a plane through the wave. Up, Up, Up we go. My back arcs, my belly is tense against the board, and my shoulders become powerful motors propelling me through the rising mass of ocean. This wave is passing all its energy to us. I can hear the wind roaring in my ears. I paddle and paddle at an incredible speed, then I grab the board with my hands and they feel so strong I could lift myself on either one of them. I stand very low and when I do it, I do not feel pain or stiffness; instead I feel power and strength. The beautiful wave starts to show its curl of spume which roars at my back like thunder. In that precise moment, when the tail of my board is pointing high up, while I am facing down the abyss of the massive ocean curl, when I softly lean towards one side to lead the board out of the mysterious hole of death and on to the adventure of life, this is when I am born again.

Upon reaching the beach, I see the sun reflecting on my skin, which looks like shiny copper. I look at my spotless hands and feel my right knee. No pain. I stretch and grab my toes with my fingers in an easy move. My lungs take in a lot of air when I breathe. It feels so good.

At my side sits the old woman except that now she is a young girl. She must be around 13 years old. For some reason I know her name is Inés.

"25 minutes", she says.

"25 minutes, what?" I ask.

"We have 25 minutes, and then we will pass on to the next life."

"Next life? What do you mean?"

"We are in the middle now. Surfers are reborn at the Portal and then go on to live their next surfer lives."

"Next life? But I am not dead yet!"

"Of course not. This must be your first time at the Portal, right?"

"Well, yeah…"

"This is my second time. But I was scared as hell on the first one. Of course, I was younger also. I

was only 65 on the first one, now I was a 69 year
old woman."
"And do you always come back this young? You
look like a 13 year old."
"13 and a half, the age when I became a surfer.
You must be close to 15."
I look at my body. My arms have not become
muscular yet. I pass my hand through my chin, no
beard. I have a permanent smile on my lips.
"Yes, it feels like 15."
"Don't you remember when you became a surfer?
Your real first ride? When you really understood the
wave and the meaning of a ride? This is your age
when you come back through the Portal. This will
be your second life ride."

Inés stands up.
"We need to start walking back now.
"But, what happens with my past life?" I ask while
standing up and wiping the sand off my butt.
"Your past life is still there; nothing has changed.
Nobody's gone, you just passed through the
Portal."

"I don't get it. I came here being 67 years old. Now I am going back being 15, what happened to the 67 year old man?"

"One surfer told me once that we are like waves. Not one, but many. We choose the life we want the same as we choose the wave we want to surf".

We start walking back; I feel confused. The beach is exactly the same as before. Nothing has changed, except for us. Nobody saw the wave, which gently took us to the shore and disappeared back into the same ocean that gave it birth. Suddenly I feel sorry for the 67 year old man that I was not anymore. Nothing this man had done in his life was extraordinary. He grew up with a single mother, had no siblings. At age 16, after a fight with his mother's boyfriend, left home to live with older friends who let him use a room in an old house close to the beach. His relationships were casual and meaningless. He never finished school and never talked to his mother again. There had been three women in his life and one son from his second girlfriend who had no contact with him. He

11

was a solitary old surfer who assumed he already had lived his best days.

"How was your past life, Inés?"

"Oh, very happy.

My Mom and Dad were very loving and I had an older sister and a brother. I went to college and was married for 45 years. I had 2 daughters and 4 lovely grandkids. My husband and I were still together when I went through the Portal. I had an extraordinary second life. But it was not like that on the first one." she hurried to say.

"How is that?" I ask.

"The first one was a selfish life. My parents were rich and I grew up living only for myself. Then I married another rich man whom I did not love. It was a miserable time. Two kids, both on drugs. One of them in jail. I became mean and resentful and hurt a lot of people. By the time I reached the Portal I was addicted to pills and had thought about killing myself."

I watch her look down at the sand and notice her blonde hair fall forward, covering part of her lovely face. She looks more childish now. Her hands are bright white and small, like her feet. She is walking fast and easy and her wet suit looks shiny and new. As I watch her, my mind feels cloudy and my memories start to fade. I try to go back and remember where I am coming from but all past experiences are turning into waves inside my head. Good feelings of love are rolling after bad feelings of selfishness. Waves of compassion crash against waves of hatred, creating infinite mixed waves from both of them. My mind has become a storm until two waves of guilt and remorse, taller than I have ever seen, break one against the other and smoothly subside altogether to become a peaceful and pristine ocean. We have reached the parking lot. I am released. I have no memories of my past life. My second life ride lays ahead of me.

The Void

Another life ride has started. Inés and I are
neighbors in the town of Jensen Beach in Florida,
where our families have become friends and enjoy
weekends together. The sun is shining on my
shoulders while we are coming out of the ocean to
eat the sandwiches our parents have prepared for
lunch. I love the time I spend with her at the beach.
We surf whenever we can, or if there are no waves,
we play with sand and talk all day long. We are
building a castle with two towers when I say:
"Hobe Sound, October 9, 2077. 25 minutes."
"What? She asks surprised."
"Oh, I don't know. Some silly date stuck in my
memory." I say.
"But, I also said the same date" said Inés. "We both
said it together."
"Hobe Sound, October 9, 2077. 25 minutes" we
both repeated at the same time and laughed.

Twenty years have passed since then. We are on
the other side of the planet, in Australia. We have

been sailing the world together for the last 5 years in our modest sailboat. Our lives are simple and fulfilled by adventure and passion. We still surf whenever we can and talk all day long. However, this day is different. This is one of those particular days that you have no more than a handful of times in your life. This is one of those days that will change you forever, like the day you marry, or the day a close relative passes away. I call these "Days of Truth".

Today, Inés is giving birth to our first son. Fatherhood starts at that very moment and I feel as proud as I can be of the family we are building. Happiness enlightens my heart in a new way.

A week later, we are both lying side by side in the forward berth of the boat with our baby placidly sleeping between us.

"What do you feel at this very moment?" Asks Inés.

"Joy." I say.

"Fulfillment." Says Inés.

We can see the stars through the open hatch at the top of our cabin and we all fall in a profound sleep while the boat rocks softly us in the protected bay of Sydney.

After the birth of our first baby, we sailed back to Jensen Beach, halfway round the world, settling back there. A total of eight "Days of Truth" have shaped our lives since then. Our marriage, three children and our parents passing away. Our family grew, lovingly caring for one another.

October 8, 2077. I am loading both surfboards in the car because tomorrow we are going surfing at Hobe Sound. . I am 81 now and Inés is 79.

"I don't know if I am going to make it tomorrow." says Inés.

"I don't know either." I say. "I am stiff as a rock. I cannot paddle fast anymore."

"My hip hurts like hell. Please remind me. Why is it that we are going?" She asks.

"We have to. That is all I know. We both have this date and place in our minds for 66 years now. We need to find out what this is about. We are soulmates, remember? That is not going to change."

Inés clutches her golden surf board pendant that I gave her in Sydney, when our first baby was born.

Every time she gets nervous, she holds and swings it right and left on its chain.

"Everything is going to be fine." I assure her.

"I love you." says Inés.

I smile back at her. We do not need words to say "I love you too".

"Hobe Sound, October 10, 2077. 25 minutes." We both say as we unload the boards in the parking lot, on the next day. We laugh together, as we did when we were teenagers and we start our walk along the beach.

After 25 minutes, we make it to the familiar spot. There are two other surfers stretching. They look younger than us, like in their sixties. One of them has a red and white long board. We start our stretching routine very slowly in silence, intrigued by the situation. I say "Hi" to the fellow with the long board. He nods at me. He is the first to go into the water. I look at Inés and we both go in together. The ocean is a little rough.

The other surfers quickly pass the breakers and sit on their boards. I feel like it is taking me ages to get there. Inés is even slower. I am breathing fast, my legs are stiff. I finally make it and wait for Inés. She arrives and passes me by without a word and goes into the deep ocean. I follow with the other two surfers. I cannot feel my hands. My paddling becomes slow and sloppy. The waves are choppy and I choke with foam. I need to stop and recover, but Inés is going too far to stop now. I do not want to leave her alone. I look back and see the beach very far away. The other surfers look back too, but we all still follow Inés. I am the last one.

Suddenly, she sits on the board and yells:
"It is coming! Go, go, go!" Inés turns her board and paddles. We are more closer to shore, so we have more time to start paddling. I am so tired already that my arms only battle the water but my speed is minimum. Inés is saying:
"Come on! You can do it! Come on!"
But still, I cannot pick up speed. I choke again and cough. I stop paddling to get air while I try to battle with my legs. I am hardly moving and the wave is already here.
"You can make it, yes you can!" I hear Inés saying.

18

I gasp for more air and when I submerge my hand in the wave my arm actually feels a strong pull. I throw in another arm and the other one feels it too. Another thrust and the board moves forward. My arms are being charged with energy as I touch the wave. I feel butterflies in my stomach.

"Go, go!" I can hear Inés.

She is already up, surfing close to me. The two other surfers are riding on the other side of the wave, also standing low. I can see their faces. They look powerful and confident.

"Now it is my time." I think. I paddle ferociously and stand up. The wave starts to roar at my back and my surfboard is pointing down. I turn my head and exchange a smile with Inés and start to lean on one side to steer the board up out of the curl. Now the wave roars and I stay low in the mist, which is blocking my sight. The swirl is all around me and I stick my left hand out to touch the internal wall of the wave to use it as a reference. The moment lasts forever. The board vibrates with speed under my feet. I cannot see. I follow the touch of my hand. There is water on my face. My body is gaining power as I surf. My breathing is strong. I feel full of

life as I re-emerge from inside the wave. I was
expelled like a rocket at the end of the curl and I
can already see the beach. I look back.

Where is Inés?

I stand tall looking for her. I see no trace of Inés.

Suddenly, I see a young surfer.

Is that her? Could that be her? I reach the beach
and look back while I stand in the shore.

Is that her?

"Inés!" I shout, "Ineees!"

The surfer turns to me and then I see the red and
white longboard.

No, that's not her!

The wave is subsiding into smaller ripples. The
other surfer appears.

I scream now "Ineeees!" And my 15 year old arms
take the surfboard back and paddle frenetically
towards the breakers.

"Help me!" I shout to the surfers, "She fell from the
wave, help me, please!"

I go into the ocean again until the beach barely
visible as a fine yellow line. No trace of her.

I have lost her.

I wander in the deep ocean looking for Inés until my memory starts to fade and my brain becomes a turbulent sea with crashing waves of remorse. It is painful to the point that I scream desperately. I am fearful because I know that in 25 minutes, when I pass to my next life, I will not not have a single memory of my soulmate and our life together.

An intense fear overcomes me that feels like I fell in a black hole. A cold sensation crawls down my back and I find it hard to breath, as if something is pressing my chest. All the beauty of the ocean is gone. The water has turned cold and the waves are dark shadows whose curls make me shiver with fear. I feel like crying but cannot articulate a sound, or a scream. In seconds, I am going to turn into nothing, and leave no trace behind me. No more existence of myself, now and never again. All of what is left of me is going to vanish. No hope. No faith. Only the void.

Hatred and Violence

25 minutes have passed. I hear a voice.

"We need to get to shore", says the young surfer with the red and white board.

"Come on, man! We will drown out here. "

"Let's go back", says the other young surfer.

I did not notice them coming and their arrival scares me as they suddenly appear at my sight.

"Uhh!" I say, looking back towards them and the shore.

"Why are we so far away? Let's go back!" I say.

We walk the beach back along together, my surf buddies and I. Our conversations are sparse and casual. I walk with my head bent down, slowly but with long strides. My permanent smile disappears. I have this constant feeling that I am missing something. My stride is that of a loner. A single date sticks to my memory: Hobe Sound, December 12, 2154. 25 minutes.

The wind is on my face. I am riding a motorcycle through the desert in Nevada twenty years later. The air comes in heat waves which are extremely intense. With my rear view, I can see the black trail of my tires in the burning asphalt. The horizon shows a blurry image of a distant mountain. I open up the zipper of my leather jacket and extract a black gun. I take out the magazine with the expert movement of my right hand and I throw it towards the desert. I keep on going for five miles and repeat the same movement with the gun.

"That's it, no murder weapon to take me to jail." I say to myself, remembering with no remorse how I shot this dealer who failed to pay me his debt. Five shots. Three for him and two for his girlfriend, whom I left alive to make an example to all other dealers.

I have been involved in drug dealing for fifteen years and you can tell when you see me that violence is a common token in my life. I stop at the next town for a sandwich. People fear guys like me because I am nothing more than an outlaw on the run, looking for cash to survive. I enter the

convenience store and I get very close to a woman who is picking up a gallon of milk from a shelf:
"If you act casual and pay for this", showing her my sandwich and a can of beer,"I will walk out without causing you any trouble." I tell her in a tense voice. She nods nervously and walks with me to the cashier. She pays for her milk and my supplies and we both walk out. Once outside I follow her up to her car. She hurries up, but I press getting closer by stretching my strides.

"You said you wouldn't cause any trouble" her voice was trembling.

I do not say a word. The moment she turns around to resist me I look at her in the eye. I can perceive her fear and feel her adrenaline running. She looks at me like begging with her eyes. I get closer and keeping my eyes on hers, I grab her right hand. Then slowly lower my hand through her fingers and without saying a word, I gently take her purse and extract her phone. I look around. No witnesses. I make a sign with my head towards her car and just say: "Go."

I wait for her to drive out and then I start driving my motorcycle in the opposite direction.

The wind is blowing in my face and thundering in my ears again. In the distance, I see red and blue lights flashing in the road.

"Damm!" I say, "they probably found the gun. How did they get me so fast? These guys have cameras in every roadway."

Two hundred yards forward, a barrier with police cars is blocking the road. It makes no sense to avoid it because they'll deactivate my motorcycle with their remote controllers. All vehicles come with this device now, which allows them to control runaways.

I bend down and grab the cables that run under the seat and pull them out, disconnecting the remote control.

"Not this motorcycle, no." I say, while pressing the accelerator and going off road into the open desert. Nobody makes an attempt to follow me. I know they will be watching my moves by satellite so they will not risk going after me by land. "I need to find a big city to hide. I'll head to Vegas where I have some friends," I think to myself.

I keep on driving in the open desert for two hours, but it is becoming too irregular. Suddenly, I see a row of rocks in front of me that looks like a thin line, darker than the rocks on the surface of the desert. Under the dark thin line a second line of rocks of a lighter color starts to show as I advance. Then, my blood freezes when I realize I am looking at a canyon, but it is too late. I cannot stop. My body feels light in the air as I fall through the air beside the cliff. For an instant I had the feeling I was on a distant beach, starting to catch a wave with my surfboard.

I feel butterflies in my stomach. Then everything went dark.

As I am dying, my memory starts to blur and my mind has turned into crashing waves. Waves of hatred combine with fear waves to dominate everything. Furious foam is flying inside my head. Then, the void is starting to show. It is a gigantic swirl that dominates the waves, making them turn, slowly at first and then frenetically fast, swallowing, through the dark center, every feeling in my personal ocean. The void devours all waves. The black hole of the swirl starts to fill up as water comes through it. As it fills in, it slows down and starts to show transparency. The waves are gone and the swirl has come to a stop. The ocean is bright and calm again.

The Wave Master

An instant later, I am on top of my surfboard. The day is sunny. I am very far away from the beach, which is visible as a thin yellow line.

I see another surfer far away, paddling deep into the ocean, and I follow instinctively.

My mind feels blurry and a warm feeling overtakes my body. Some memories start to come back to me. "Could that be her?" I think to myself.

I paddle faster and am getting closer. I do not dare call her name. I can see her blonde hair now. I paddle a little more and reach for her. When I touch her shoulder it seems to me like somebody else takes her place and turns. I am shocked. He looks at me and I cannot help but ask, surprised:

"Who are you?"

His answer is paused and calm:

"I am the Wave Master." he says.

I am confused and start throwing questions at him.

"The Wave Master?

And what does that mean?

Where are we?"

He looks around.

"Don't you recognize the place? We are at the Portal." says the Wave Master.

My mind lights up, and suddenly I remember everything. My past lives, my parents, my wife and my kids, the people I loved and the ones I hurt. The first time I went through the Portal, and my soul mate, Inés. Then the void, the violence and the hatred.

"Why are we here?" I ask.

"All surfers come here to take their next life ride."

"But, where do we go when we die? Because I died, didn't I?"

"When we die, nothing gets lost. We simply go back to the ocean and ride another wave."

"Another wave? Just like that? But what happens to all these people we have been, do they go to heaven or hell, or somewhere?" My voice reaches a high pitch.

"You see, we are all of the versions of ourselves at the same time, but the Portal lets you go from one version to another. Imagine that you, and everything that surrounds you is composed of waves. These waves have different characteristics. Some are tall and crisp, some are low and round, you pick the wave to ride that suits your vision of life. We choose to ride a certain wave, or live a certain life, but they all coexist, it's just our vision that changes.

The Portal simply allows you to change your vision and ride another life."

"Like a second chance?" I ask.

"Like a second, a third, and an infinite number of chances." he answers.

"And they all coexist? Like at the same time? How is that possible?"

"Humans and things. Everything that surrounds us is part of this ocean. We just do not understand most of what happens to us and therefore we order it in a time sequence. But when we do this, we also separate ourselves from the rest by classifying our environment. We classify what has happened as an irrevocable fact. We separate the ones who lived in a certain way from others who have acted differently.

Past, present and future help us align actions and consequences to satisfy our reasoning. However, the only one that is real is the present, what is happening now. Past and future are inventions of our minds."

I stare at the blue horizon while thinking on the times I have condemned myself for things I have done in the past. At all those times, I have felt divided and unloved. I feel guilt.

"And is this true for everybody, no matter how good or bad we have been in our past life?" I ask.

"You need to learn to love every version of yourself, when you do that, you will understand there is no difference between loving yourself and loving every other being. We are all one. The good ones and the bad ones are the same. Doing something good for someone is doing good for everyone.

This is the same at all levels." continued the Wave Master.

"To separate nature from human beings, or to distinguish ourselves by characteristics of each one is in essence not accepting that we are all one, that we all share the same existence. When we

31

separate ourselves from others we stop loving the
ocean.

"And what about love?" I asked suddenly
remembering Inés and longing for a second
chance.
"Love is what keeps all this together." says the
Wave Master.
"We really learn to love when we accept all
versions of ourselves and others."
He paused.
"You can only fall in love with a wave when you are
in love with the ocean."

"So if this universe is made of waves, who are
you?"
"Come closer and ask me again."
I paddle towards him and look him in the eye.
"Who are you?"
"Ask me again."
"Who are you?"
"Ask me again."
"Who are you? But, aren't you going to respond?"
"It's not the answer that matters, it is the question."

32

As we stare in silence I notice how familiar he looks
to me.
He must be no more than 15 years old.
Not muscular yet. No beard.
He has a permanent smile on his lips.

I hear a distant voice calling.
"Its coming!
Come on! Start paddling. Quick!" she urges me and
paddles sideways. "It will break that way."
I follow.
"It is breaking!
Go, go, go!"
I feel the energy of the wave pushing through the
water.
My board speeds up towards her.
Each time I touch the water a shock of energy
pases through my body and shakes me up all the
way to my toes. The wave elevates us and starts to
roar at our backs. I can feel the wind on my face
when I grab the board and stand up low. Our
boards are now pointing down to the abyss of this
tremendous ocean curl. I turn my head and smile at

Inés, whose smile says "I love you too" with no words. We both lean slowly out of the curl and looking into each other's eyes, we steer our boards to the adventure of another surfer life.

Epilogue

We are at the beach together, but this time my skin is not shiny like copper. My hands are spotted with freckles and Inés' hair is white.

We have a "Moment of Truth".

While sitting in the sand, Inés is looking at me and the sun is reflecting in her white hair.

"We do not have 25 minutes. We have all the time in the world." I say.

"You know," she says, her voice charged with emotion, "we do not need the Portal."

"We do not need the wave either, even we do not need to surf." I say.

She turns and looks at the placid blue ocean.

"If we decide to live another life we only need to leave our experiences behind and be brave enough to ride the new adventure, to change," Inés responds.

"We are the choice of what we decide now, no matter what or where we are." I say,

"The secret is...Life is an eternal Portal."